Sexy Surprises for Christmas

Sexy Surprises, Volume 30

Giselle Renarde

Published by Giselle Renarde, 2023.

Table of Contents

Sexy Surprises
for Christmas

6 Erotic Stories
Giselle Renarde

One Wild Christmas Party

L ast year, Lars gave me the silliest Christmas gift: crotchless panties with a silky sprig of mistletoe hanging right over the clit.

Actually, he got himself a pair too. His were a little different, obviously. Instead of a strip of crotchlessness, Lars's mistletoe undies had a hole cut out in the front for his dick to poke through. He'd walked into the living room wearing just that ridiculous thong with his hard cock sticking out, and I had no choice but give him the world's best blowjob right there beside the Christmas tree.

When I put on my pair, he took me upstairs and kissed my pussy until I couldn't breathe.

After that, the *his-and-hers* undies sunk to the bottom of the laundry hamper with the rest of the "handwash only" stuff. I'd totally forgotten about them until I came home from work to find the silly things hanging over the towel bar.

"I washed them in the sink," Lars told me. "I thought we could wear them tonight."

My jaw clenched because I figured he'd forgotten about Ravinia and Stone's Christmas party. It bugged the hell out of me when I told him something forty times and he was still like, "Duh... what?"

But Lars hadn't forgotten. Not at all. He wanted us to wear the mistletoe unties to the party.

"But your dick!" I cried, which made me giggle even though I was trying to be serious. "Your dick hangs right out of those things. There's no support. People will stare at you! They'll point at your crotch and say, 'Look at that! Lars isn't wearing any underwear.'"

"Nobody's going to stare at my crotch," he said. "And even if they do, so what? They can look, but they can't touch."

That made me laugh out loud, and I picked up my crotchless panties from the towel bar. They were made of that silky-stretchy material that dries really fast, so they were just about ready to slip on.

"I was going to wear that short red dress, the clingy jersey one." I held the panties up against me. "What if I open my legs a little too wide and somebody gets a peek at my pink?"

Lars came close. He wrapped his arms around me and kissed my forehead. "They can look, but they can't touch."

I bent my head up and kissed Lars's lips, and that kiss drew itself out and dragged us into the bedroom. Lars leaned against the headboard and I leaned against his hard body, running my hands up and down his back. It didn't seem to matter how long we were together. He always turned me on. Always.

But when I reached down to cup his package, Lars grabbed my wrist and held my hand away. "Not yet," he said. "I want you good and horny at this party."

I gulped. "Why?"

"Because," he said. "I want you willing to do things you wouldn't normally do."

My heart pounded against my ribcage. It was all I could hear. I didn't know what my man had in store for me, but I couldn't wait to find out.

Ravinia's place was hopping when we got there. Just a house party, but those were the best at Christmas time. You could get good and drunk and know there was always a couch to crash on.

The stereo blasted out a collection of funky Christmas tunes recorded by Mr. Tall Dark and Handsome himself, Ravinia's super-hot boyfriend Stone. "As in Stone Cold Fox," I'd said to Lars when we'd first met him.

Lars had said, "I think it's more like a tribute to Sly and the Family Stone."

And, judging by his music, Lars was probably right.

But so was I, because Stone was foxy with a capital F.

I giggled when he brought me my fifth glass of egg nog.

"What's so funny?" Stone asked, taking the seat across from mine. I was clinging dizzily to the couch. Even though I was sitting down, I still felt like I could either fall over or float away. I wasn't sure which.

"I don't know why I'm laughing," I said. "Must be the rum."

"Ahh..." Stone nodded, smiley and joyful as ever.

And then, suddenly, something changed.

His grin fell and his eyes glowed with a darkness I'd never seen in him before. I thought maybe I'd done or said something to offend him, and all at once I felt too sober for my own good.

Then I followed his gaze down, and I realized what he was seeing.

I'd forgotten myself and spread my legs. My short dress parted at my thighs. There wasn't enough fabric to hang between them and block his view of my pussy. He was looking at it, staring at my hot pink centre. Could he see how wet I was from drinking and flirting with other men while Lars looked on, grinning wolfishly, enjoying my lust? I bet Stone could even see how hard my fat little clit ached to be sucked, teased, toyed with.

Lars had gotten his wish. I was horny and ready for anything.

A slapping sound whipped through the air, drawing my attention away from Stone. I snapped my legs together as I looked around the room, thinking something had fallen or... well, I didn't know what.

There was Lars in an antique rocking chair. He'd take Ravinia across his lap and pulled up the skirt on her sexy Santa outfit—one of those fuzzy red numbers lined with white fluff.

He'd smacked her ass, and he did it again. My man brought his big palm down across our friend's tight little bum. She had on red panties that probably came with the outfit, and she shrieked when Lars pulled them down. Everybody who hadn't already been looking turned to see my Lars spanking Ravinia's red bottom.

Slap, slap, slap.

The sound was almost as loud as her squeals of, "No, Lars, stop!"

But it was hard to take her seriously when she giggled after every word.

"I hope somebody's taking pictures," Lars said.

Stone already had his phone out. "Don't worry, mate. I'm getting it all on film."

"This could be your big break!" somebody shouted from across the room.

"You're going to be a star of the internet porn sites, Ravinia!"

Everybody teased and taunted her while my man smacked her ass. She writhed in his lap, not enough to escape, but enough that her ample cleavage threatened to fall from her Santa Girl top, which was little more than a bra with red sleeves. She's worn her dark hair in pigtails which bobbed in the air every time Lars smacked her. I kept staring at her tits, hoping they'd fall loose from that top and I'd get to see her nipples. I don't know why I wanted to, but I did.

"Show her what's under the mistletoe, Lars!"

It wasn't until half the room had turned to look at me that I realized I'd spoken. In a way, I couldn't believe it. I felt outside of myself, like someone else had taken over my body. I was possessed by the Ghost of Christmas Sexy.

"What's under the mistletoe?" asked a woman in a sheer gold dress.

Lars stopped smacking Ravinia's ass. He looked around the room at the audience he'd drawn.

"Yeah, Lars," Ravinia said. "I want to see what's under the mistletoe."

She could probably feel it pressing into her side, the way she was slumped over his lap.

"Jess?" Lars looked to me and I bit my lip to contain my excitement. "You insist?"

I could feel a few pairs of eyes burning into the back of my neck, but they belonged to people who didn't know I was a share bear extraordinaire. If they were waiting for an explosion of jealousy from yours truly, they'd better sit back and watch the show.

"I insist," I said with a resolute nod. I winked, just to show I was extra okay with this.

SEXY SURPRISES FOR CHRISTMAS

"How about I show Ravinia my mistletoe if you show Stone yours?"

A blush came over me because, of course, Stone had already seen it. *And* because I'd never lifted my skirt before a live studio audience.

But I said, "Okay. It's a deal."

Ravinia shuffled off Lars's lap and he stood while she kneeled before him. The whole room watched him take off his festive red-white-and-green checked shirt. His clothes looked so normal, with only his 1980's *A Flock Of Seagulls* hairstyle betraying his rampant freakishness.

I remembered how opposed I'd been to us wearing our mistletoe out tonight, and felt silly about that strange bout of prudishness.

When Lars pushed down his grey trousers, the crowd issued a collective gasp, which made me laugh. The party people laughed, too, though I could still feel a few eyes burning into the back of my head.

"My god, what is that?" Ravinia asked.

Everybody laughed and Lars said, "Well, it's not a fruitcake, but have a little taste. You just might like it."

His cock was hard as steel. Nothing unusual there, but it did look pretty funny sticking out of the hole in that ridiculous thong.

"Are you one of Santa's elves?" Ravinia asked Lars's cock as it bounced joyfully in front of her face.

"Are *you*?" Lars shot back at Ravinia.

"You're certainly dressed the part," someone said from across the room. Her silly red top was tumbling off one shoulder.

The tension in the air was fierce, so thick and hot it was streaming up the windows. Outside, big balls of snow fluttered from the sky. Indoors, the heat was almost unbearable. There were so many people in this room, all focused on Ravinia's mouth as it wrapped itself around Lars's thick cock. They both moaned when she sucked it, but the rest of the room went dead silent. People collectively held their breath. You could feel it. Even I didn't want to breathe for fear of making some noise that might bring this debauchery to a close.

Ravinia wrapped her fingers around my man's shaft and made a fist. She pumped it against her closed lips, pressed right up against his cockhead like she was giving it a Christmas kiss.

"That's what mistletoe's for!" said a drunk man, someone I think I slept with at one of these parties. But that was a long time ago. And we'd done it under a pile of coats, not right out in the open.

"Lars," I said, and he gazed right at me. "Look at her lips. They're almost as red as your cock."

He looked down. His smile grew as Ravinia planted sharp red kisses up and down his shaft. I wanted to do that too. I wanted to kiss Lars's cock with her, and before I knew it I was stumbling off the couch and crawling across the carpet, lusting after my man's hard dick.

Ravinia was already kneeling between his legs, so I hugged his thigh and wrapped my mouth around the base of his cock. I bit his dick and he groaned, running a hand through my hair, encouraging more. I knew what Lars liked, and Ravinia knew what everyone liked. She sucked the tip of his cock, just the tip, between those cherry-red lips while I planted slobbery kisses all over his shaft.

SEXY SURPRISES FOR CHRISTMAS

I could never believe how hot his cock got when he was turned on. It was a missile, live ammunition ready to launch. I knew what would put him over the top. While Ravinia devoured my man, taking his dick deep in her throat, I plucked his balls out through the tight elastic hole in his thong.

"Fuuuck," Lars moaned, and I could hear other partygoers breathing heavily, almost panting, behind me. I wondered if they could see my ass, or perhaps my crotchless panties. If not, they would soon enough.

Bowing between Lars's legs, I sucked his balls, carefully at first, building up pressure as I went. Ravinia made kittenish mewling sounds, and I made them too, because my man's salty, sweaty balls tasted even better than Ravinia's goat cheese and fig pastries. Even better than her lipstick, which was all over my man's dick.

"I'm gonna come," Lars warned us, and I could feel it in his body. His balls got so tight I could fit them in my mouth, both at once. I sucked them hard and Lars yelped my name. At first I thought I'd hurt him, but then, when Ravinia started sputtering, I realized he'd just filled her throat with cream. It was always a never-ending flow with Lars. He just kept coming and coming, and all you could do was open your throat and make room for it.

"Fuck," he said, stumbling across the room and taking the seat I'd abandoned on the couch. His cock was still half hard, coming to a rest on the pillow of his balls. The silky red mistletoe sat atop his dick like the star on a Christmas tree, greeting the room with the possibilities it had opened up.

"Your turn, Jess." Lars looked at me and winked. "Give the people what they want. Show them *your* mistletoe."

The air in the room filled with sexual tension so thick I could barely breathe. All at once, it broke into a chant of, "Show us, show us, show us!"

So I closed my eyes and lifted my skirt. There was a collective silence in the room, and I knew everybody was looking at me. Everyone could see the place where my panties split in the middle... but they couldn't see enough.

Feeling my way down, I sat in the rocking chair and opened my legs. The silence deepened as everyone got a look at the glistening pink of me.

Crotchless panties sure were a crowd-pleaser. The room started chanting "Eat her! Eat her!" and I felt Stone's mass between my legs. He was all heat, that man, like a furnace. When I opened my eyes, there he was, grinning like a demon. He asked me if I was ready and I said, "Isn't it obvious?"

He asked again and I simply said yes.

I closed my eyes, feeling dizzy and sleepy, but at the same time very alert. I heard the rustle of his clothes as he drew in close. In my mind, I kept seeing his dark eyes, his lust. And then, for some reason, I knew I had to find Lars. My eyes shot open and I spotted him on the couch, watching, seeming worn out and amorous and amused all at one.

"Lucky you," he said with just his lips, no sound.

Or maybe that was, "Love you."

I smiled, so distracted that I really wasn't ready when Stone's lips met my clit. I started to jump, but he caught my bare thighs with both hands and pressed them into the rocking chair.

His lips were unbelievably hot.

Stone held me in that chair, which creaked with every pitch forward and back. He followed my body with his, moving with my pussy as the rocker swayed. His lips remained closed and pressed against my clit, but my flesh was so swollen and ready that the mere pressure worked me quickly toward climax. I could feel my orgasm sitting in my belly like a ball of fire, waiting for something to set it off.

"Suck her clit," Lars said, which sure enough started a new chant.

The whole room joined in, like a Christmas carol: "Suck her clit! Suck her clit!"

"But it's mistletoe on her panties," Stone argued, grinning wickedly. "You don't suck a woman under the mistletoe, you kiss her!"

The room was adamant: "Suck it! Suck it! Suck it!"

I'd never had an entire Christmas party cheering for my clit to get sucked. I felt like I should be embarrassed, but I guess I was drunk enough to find everything hilarious. Even the sensation of Stone's sizzling lips against my bare pussy made me snicker.

Stone gazed up at me like a pouting puppy. "You want me to suck your clit, Jessie?"

I giggled, and when I tried to stop I just giggled louder.

"Is that a yes?" he asked.

God, his voice was sexy—velvet gravel, liquid sex.

I nodded jubilantly, laughing until he wrapped his mouth around my fat little clit and started to suck. Arching in the rocker, I grabbed the armrests with both hands. If my nails had been longer, I'd have dug them into the wood, leaving permanent scars. I couldn't believe how immediate the wave came over me, shrouding my body in the tingling warmth of orgasm. It was centred in my clit, but the heat of his mouth radiated out from there, filling my belly with fire, making my nipples hard under my bra.

My climax took over as Stone sucked my clit. I could feel it in my scalp, in my fingertips, needles and heat. Frenzy surged through me, like I had to shake the sensation out. I started writhing in the rocking chair, hoping to god I wouldn't break the spindled wood.

I wrapped my legs around Stone's head, bucking my wet pussy against his face. I could feel how soaked my panties had become, absorbing the juice of my arousal as it slipped down my crack. Stone's lips splayed mine, and I came even harder watching him savour my cunt.

Then, out of nowhere, Lars and Ravinia opened my red dress and heaved my breasts from my bra. When their mouths found my nipples, my body exploded. It was fireworks everywhere, exploding in the three mouths latched firmly to my flesh.

They held me down as I writhed. Over my screams, I could just hear the room cheering me on, telling me to come harder, scream louder. Everyone was so close, peering over Lars and Ravinia's heads, trying to get a better look at my tits.

Their eyes were everywhere. I could feel them like fingers dancing across my skin, leaving traces of communal lust. Everybody wanted me. Everybody had me, vicariously, through Stone's mouth, and Lars's and Ravinia's.

When I couldn't stand any more, they had mercy. I slid from the rocking chair like liquid and slumped into a puddle on the floor. My legs were open. In my soaked crotchless panties, I could feel the warm air from the heater right against my naked pussy. My dress was open too, and my boobs spilled out over the cups of my bra, my nipples pointing up at the ceiling.

SEXY SURPRISES FOR CHRISTMAS

I could feel Stone sitting beside me. I could hear Lars and Ravinia talking, but I only listened to the tenor of their voices, not to the words they were saying.

Closing my eyes, I made myself into art—something to be looked at, and maybe even touched if you were sneaky. Everyone could see me now, see my naked breasts, see the gape of my pussy and my exhausted clit under the mistletoe.

And to think I didn't want us wearing our crotchless undies to the Christmas party. We'd have missed out on all this. Instead, we'd shared ourselves with everyone, and the memory made me smile so wide my cheeks hurt.

Love It or Love It

"WHAT DO YOU WANT FOR Christmas?"

"Ugh. Nothing. I don't know." Lili flopped on the couch, sending clouds of cat hair into the air. Snuggie jumped on top of her and started kneading her belly. Petting his ginger neck, she asked, "Do we really need to celebrate Christmas *every* year? I'm just about done with holidays. What a waste of time."

I took two steps away to show her I was *literally* taken aback. "You're kidding, right?"

"And money," she added. "Christmastime is such a drain. I don't see what you get out of it, Nor."

"You mean beyond the fact that if it wasn't for the mad, frantic Christmastime mentality we'd never have met?"

A smile broke slowly across Lili's lips. "True."

She didn't say anything as Snuggie made her belly his own personal cat bed. When she closed her eyes I knew she was remembering the day we met, remembering the *way* we met. So I turned up the Christmas music on the radio and I lifted her shoes from her feet and sat at the end of the couch to rub her ice-cold toes.

"Chilly out there today," I said.

"It was a beautiful day, the day we met. Those big fluffy snowballs, mild weather." Lili smiled. "There was supposed to be a blizzard, I remember, so I hadn't planned on going shopping."

"Same here, which stressed me out of my mind because I had a million stupid things to buy."

"Me too," Lili said with a laugh. "I thought I'd be super-aunt and get my nephew whatever the hot toy was that year."

"I believe it was *Tickle My Asshole*."

Lili cracked up so hard Snuggie momentarily considered dismounting. She kicked my thigh and said, "You're terrible."

"Well, I only remember because I was trying to snag one too, for my ex's daughter."

Looking past Snuggie, Lili cocked her head and said, "You never told me that."

"Really?" And here I thought I'd told her everything. "Yeah, I wanted her to see how mature and understanding I was, even though I'd never felt so spurned."

"Ahh." Lili closed her eyes and took a deep breath. "So if it hadn't been for rabid consumerism, we'd never have met."

"Nope." Wrapping my hands around one woolly sock, I massaged Lili's foot until she moaned. "Remember how mad you were?"

Her eyes shot open. "How mad *I* was? *You* were the one foaming at the mouth. I thought you had rabies for a second."

"I think I was entitled to be a little upset. The accident was your fault, after all."

Lili probably would have shot straight up if it hadn't been for the cat on her stomach. "The accident was not my fault."

I laughed to keep it light. We'd had this argument too many times. Now it had dwindled down to a funny story we told our friends—unless one or both of us was in a bad mood, in which case it turned back into an argument.

My laughter was infectious, apparently, because Lili said, "Yeah okay, it was mostly my fault."

"Mostly?"

"Yes, mostly."

That yes was pretty sharp, so I backed off. "I probably shouldn't have been driving so fast in a parking lot—you've got me there."

"And I should have been extra sure there was nobody behind me when I backed out of that spot."

"I couldn't figure out why you were doing that," I told her. "You'd just beaten me to it, then suddenly you were backing out again?"

"I wasn't straight," Lili said.

"Yeah, no kidding."

"My *car* wasn't straight." She opened her eyes just so she could roll them. "I had to back up to straighten it out."

Reflecting on what definitely did not feel like a meet-cute at the time, I said, "I hit you and I felt it. I *felt* it, *then* heard the crash. Must have been your tail light shattering, but I don't know what I thought it was at the time. I remember having this overwhelming feeling like I was about to be in so much trouble."

"You were."

"You were indignant," I told her, laughing.

"We both were: we tore out of our cars, slammed the doors and let 'er rip! I don't think I'd ever sworn at a stranger before."

That seemed unlikely. "For being unpracticed, you sure had a knack for it."

"Thanks," Lili said. "You weren't so bad yourself."

"We were so in each other's face," I recalled. "I don't think I even looked at you until ten minutes into our battle. You were just a blur in a baby blue pea jacket."

"Yup, and you were a scary street tough. I had to puff up my chest to show I wasn't afraid."

"Afraid of me?" I mocked being taken aback, but kept on squeezing her toes. "I was a pussycat. You just didn't know it yet."

For a moment, we reflected in silence.

"Then you invited me into your car to exchange insurance information," Lili said. "And all I kept thinking was how glad I was you weren't a man."

That deserved a half-laugh. "Yeah, no kidding. I had no idea what we were supposed to do. I'd never been in an accident."

"Same. Remember I told you I was calling the police?"

"I think I said the same."

"Probably." She sighed. "Then I got into your car and you had that little heart-shaped rainbow flag medallion handing from your mirror."

"My ex gave me that," I told her. "Good thing I never took it down."

"No kidding. Because when I saw that, I actually looked at you for the first time. I looked at your face and I liked it."

I rolled my eyes. "God only knows why."

"I know why." Lili started to sit up, but Snuggie growled. "It was your nose, in particular. I'd never seen a nose quite like it."

"What's so great about my nose?"

"I can't describe it," she said, wistfully. "I just really liked it. And your hair, too. When you took your hat off it stuck out everywhere. You looked like the kid in the Science Centre poster with his hand on that electricity ball."

"Thanks," I groaned.

"Yeah, but it humanized you, see? You weren't the bad guy anymore."

"That's how I felt about your cold sore," I confessed. "I'd just gotten over one, so when I noticed it on your top lip I remember feeling bad for you. I knew how much it must hurt."

"Yeah, you said that," Lili reminded me. "In the car, you said that. It made me self-conscious."

"No need to feel that way," I assured her. "I thought you were gorgeous. Like, POW, there's a beautiful woman in your car. What do you do?"

Lili kicked me. "Flatterer."

"Not even. And I felt guilty for a second because I thought you were like a sixteen-year-old kid. Then you took out your license and I snuck a peek at your birthday and, my god, was I ever relieved. Still, hard to believe you were almost thirty. You looked like a teenager. You still do, in fact."

Lili rolled her eyes, but didn't go so far as to accuse me of empty flattery. She knew she still looked incredibly young. "And then cars started honking at us," she said, "because we were blocking the roadway or whatever you call it. And you said you couldn't find some document: *it must be at home*."

"Which was a total lie," I admitted.

"Because it took you a grand total of fourteen seconds after I'd sat my ass down in your car before you decided you had to get in my pants."

"Well..."

"Well?"

"Yeah."

"Heh." Lili scratched Snuggie behind his ears, which only seemed to annoy him. "I can't believe how stupid I was."

"Stupid how?"

"Well, you told me you lived nearby. You said I could leave my car at the mall and you'd drive me to your nice warm house. We could have a hot chocolate and go through the paperwork, then you'd deliver me back to the parking lot. And I go, 'Sure! Let's do it!' I'm like that one character in the horror movie where you'd saying, 'Don't get in the car! Don't get in the car!' and, sure enough, she gets in the car."

"Lucky for you I wasn't a serial killer."

"Lucky for you I was horny." Lili raised an eyebrow, then poked her toe at the crotch of my jeans. "I could tell you were a sure thing."

"Yeah right." Not sure why I was arguing. "I thought you were too pretty to be queer. Talk about a femmephobe, eh? I figured you had to be straight, *had to be*. And then you go peeking around my house, sticking your head in my bedroom..."

"I'm embarrassed just thinking about it." Lili covered her face with both hands to illustrate her level of embarrassment.

"You ask to use the bathroom and, yeah, of course you can. So I go into the kitchen and put on the kettle, and when you come out your pants are gone."

"Don't remind me!"

"And all you've got on are these plaid knee socks."

"Argyle," she said. "Not plaid."

"And this pink sweater..."

"*Salmon* sweater."

"...that barely covers your cooch, and you don't even explain your pantlessness to me. You've just suddenly got no pants, and you hop on my table and I see you've got no underwear either."

Lili shrugged. "Ahh, to be young again."

"So you're sitting on my table and I'm thinking, 'Thank god that thing is oak' because some tables, you know, you sit on it and you fall right through. But you're sitting on my table wearing this sweater and these socks and you've got your legs open just slightly, just enough, and I'm working out what you want me to do."

"Wasn't it obvious?" Lili asked, dubiously. "I wanted you to sit in that chair between my legs just go at me."

"Well, that's what I did."

"Yeah."

When Lili stopped at "Yeah," I asked, "What?"

"Nothing."

"I just thought you'd be..."

"What?"

"More excited about it."

"*More excited about it?* I was scared as hell. I thought it's what you wanted, but you were a stranger."

"A stranger sitting on your kitchen table in no panties."

"In no pants."

"Well, exactly."

All these years Lili thought I could have been more excited, did she? She obviously had no idea what the sight of her did for me back then, and what it still does for me now. Lili never stopped being gorgeous. Christmas after Christmas, she grew more beautiful, more confident, more kinky and more *mine*.

I bolted from the couch and Snuggie followed suit, racing from the room as Lili asked, "Where's the fire?"

"In my pants." I dropped them and she cracked up. "This is no laughing matter, Lili. Do you know who bad I want you?"

"No."

Neither did I, since I'd kind of summoned this arousal out of nowhere. Somehow I thought that if I showed her how excited she got me now, she'd realize I was just as excited the day we met. So, hiking her up off the couch, I pulled down her pants and dragged her—puzzled, but not exactly kicking and screaming—to the same oak table, now in our dining room.

"What are you doing?" Once she started laughing, she couldn't stop. "Nora, this is silly."

"You're silly," I shot back. "Now show me that pretty pink pussy."

When she was pantless, I picked her up, placed her on the table, and opened her smooth shaved legs. I left on the woolly socks. Didn't want her feet getting cold.

Just as she'd done the day we first met, Lili asked, "Do you want this top off or on?"

"Off," I growled, and the moment she exposed her breasts to the cool winter air, I reached the heady realms I'd been seeking. "God, I love this pert little body."

Throwing myself at her breast, I took a nipple in my mouth and sucked. I loved that texture on my tongue, like a nice fat Goodies candy. I loved the way it moved against my tongue as I licked it, and I loved the way she panted and moaned and pleaded, "Not so hard, Nor! It hurts!"

I couldn't help myself. I switched to the other tit and licked that, trying to restrain myself, but it was impossible. I sucked that one too, hard enough to make my honey screech and kick her feet in the air. She pulled away, fighting me until her back met the table.

"God, Lili." I ran my hands through my short hair. I didn't know where to begin with that body, that body laid out for me like a holiday feast. "God, you're gorgeous!"

My palm decided for me, pressing into her pussy, rubbing that slick surface until Lili whimpered. She covered her breasts, maybe to protect them from the cold or to protect them from me, but when I shoved two fingers in her cunt she broke down and started toying with her tits. She flinched every time she squeezed them, probably because they were so tender from how hard I'd sucked. Maybe I should have felt bad, but I didn't. I could hear in her shallow breaths how much she loved it when I roughed her up.

"My clit," she gasped. "Nor, come on."

"Come on what?" I teased.

She started bucking her hips, picking her ass up off the table and trying to get me to do something. "My clit. Stroke my clit."

"Stroke it?" I asked as I fucked her with my fingers."

"Stroke it, yeah."

"Or lick it?"

"Yeah, lick it!" Shrieking, she held her breasts hard against her chest, like she worried they might fall off. "Lick it. Oh god, please, Nora. Please lick my clit. Please lick it."

I didn't want to take my fingers out of her warm, tight cunt, but going down with them inside her always felt messy and awkward. So I picked up one of the beeswax candlesticks that lived in the holder without ever getting lit, and I shoved that inside her while I bowed between her legs.

"Nora!" she screamed, trying to get a look. "Did you grow a cock?"

"I wish!"

She asked, "What did you put in me?"

"I'll never tell," I said, playing, trying to block her view of the candlestick. "Next time you'll have to pay closer attention."

"I can't," she cried as I licked her engorged clit with the tip of my tongue. "I can't. You make me crazy. You make me wild. My brain goes out the window."

"I know how you feel," I agreed. "It's not every day I bring home strangers and eat them on my kitchen table."

Felt like only yesterday, but it also felt like a million years ago.

"Not too hard, Nor." Lili's pussy muscles tightened around the candle. I could hardly move it, so I just tried harder. "Oh my god, what you do to me..."

I couldn't speak. My mouth was busy making sweet love to her pink parts. The candle rubbed against my chin as I sucked her clit, making a comical *eee-err* sound with every thrust. Even that couldn't crack me up. I was lost in the moment—in *our* moment, in reliving the day we'd met after a low-speed collision in a shopping mall parking lot.

"I'm gonna come, Nor!" She raised her hips and grabbed her ass cheeks, pulling them apart so far I wished I had a slimmer candle to shove up that chute. She'd probably kick me in the nose if I tried. "Suck my clit, Nora. I'm gonna come! I'm gonna come so haaaaaard!"

That vowel stretched into eternity, and then spun off into a scream. She bucked at the candle and fucked at my face, banging her pelvic bone into my upper lip, which smashed painfully against my teeth. Anything for my girl.

"Oh my god, Nora, I can't even breathe. I can't even... oh my GOD!"

Pulling the candle from her pussy, I said, "How's that for excitement?"

Lili rolled onto her side, and then back on her back. She was panting and moaning, writhing like her body was reliving that orgasm over and over again.

"I love getting you off," I told her.

"You're pretty damn good at it, I gotta say."

"I love that you let me."

"Anytime," she said with a breathless chuckle.

I sat back and absentmindedly licked the candle I'd used to fuck her. It tasted like Lili's musk coupled with the sweetness of honey. Perfect dessert, and we hadn't even started dinner yet.

"The day we met," Lili said, still panting. "I was so mad at you. The accident and your anger, they got me so riled up. I hadn't felt like that in... I don't know how long. You got me so worked up. That's why I wanted you."

"You wanted me because I pissed you off?" I said between languorous licks at the candle.

With her eyes closed, she said, "Nobody else had brought out that kind of emotion in me, not since I was a teenager. I felt young with you. Angry, sure, but I'd shut so much of myself down after my first girlfriend left me. I never wanted to feel that way again."

"If you don't want to be hurt, don't fall in love," I said.

With her eyes full of tears, she said, "I fell in love with you, Nora. I knew it right from the start."

"I knew it too," I told her. "Maybe not from the moment our tail light smashed my headlight, but... soon thereafter."

Lili sat up on the table, looking gorgeous and glowing and blissfully exhausted. "Okay, you win. Christmas forever."

A Threesome for Christmas

"You're heck of a lot younger than most of the clients see."

That was pretty much the first thing the bathtub installe told her when he arrived at her house.

Cathy blushed, even though it was hardly a compliment "The new tub is for my mother. She's coming for Christmas.. and staying forever."

He cocked his brow.

"She's moving in with me," Cathy clarified.

"Well, isn't that nice?" the installer said.

Cathy had already forgotten his name. Isn't that awful?

"It'll be an adjustment, that's for sure." Suddenly, she fel self-conscious, standing in the bathroom with a perfect stranger "Can I get you a coffee or anything? A cup of tea? I've got bacon in the fridge, if you want eggs and toast. Oh, but I only have ry bread. I know some people find the flavour a little strong..."

When the installer man smiled, Cathy's knees turned to jelly

"Don't you worry about me," he said. "I'll just get to work on this tub and hopefully be out of your hair by five."

Five. Five o'clock. Five o'clock shadow.

Chiseled jaw. Broad shoulders. Tight butt.

Stop!

Cathy smiled so hard her cheeks hurt.

Nodding, she backed out of the bathroom.

She felt like an idiot, especially when she caught Jeremy staring at her from the basement door.

"Jeremy!" she shrieked. "You nearly scared the pants off me."

He raised an eyebrow and she felt another blush coming on. She was so flustered this morning. What was wrong with her?

"So, what's going on up here?" Jeremy asked.

He had a cup of coffee in hand, which was about all he ever prepared in his kitchenette downstairs. Whenever he wanted to cook "real food" he used her kitchen on the main floor—which was just as well, since Cathy hated cooking and he always made extra.

"The bath installer," Cathy said. "Remember? I'm having one of those special tubs put in for my mother."

"Pricey Christmas gift," Jeremy said.

Cathy rolled her eyes. "Don't get me started."

She walked into the kitchen, hyper-conscious of every word that came out of her mouth. It made her nervous, knowing that what's-his-name, the installer with the square jaw and muscles of steel, could hear their conversation. What would he think of her, living with a young man? Maybe he'd think Jeremy was her son. She almost hoped he would think that, even though the truth wasn't so sensational.

"What's so special about this new bathtub?" Jeremy asked, following Cathy into the kitchen. "The old one looked fine to me."

He set his coffee cup on her table and rifled through her newspaper.

"It'll be easier for Mom to get in and out of," Cathy said. She sat, but at the edge of her chair. "Haven't you seen those commercials? They're good for older people, so they don't have to step up and risk falling. The tub itself is higher than normal, but it has a watertight door. You can either shower in it or sit on the ledge and take a bath."

"That's good, I guess." Jeremy didn't seem to be listening, but maybe he was. She always found it hard to tell with him. "But why spend the money? Couldn't you just help your mom in and out of the bath?"

A familiar sourness planted itself in the pit of Cathy's stomach. "Would you want to help your mother bathe?"

Jeremy turned up his nose. "I see your point."

Hot tears welled in Cathy's eyes. Shifting out of her chair, she turned toward the sink because she didn't want Jeremy to see her cry. She grabbed the kettle and dumped out the stale water, adding fresh, then turning it on. What else could she do? Wash her breakfast dishes. That would buy her enough time for the choking sensation in her throat to subside.

But Jeremy wasn't a stupid guy. He said, "Hey Cath, what's wrong? Anything I can do?"

How could she answer a question like that? Her shoulders fell, followed by her head, and she told him, "There's nothing anyone can do. Not only am I alone, but now I get to spend the next few years of my life playing nursemaid to a mother who thinks everything I do is wrong. I don't want to do this, Jeremy! I don't want her living here!"

When Cathy turned, Jeremy was right there in front of her, ready for her to collapse in his arms. And she did. She'd been holding in her tears for too long, and they all came out, soaking his terrycloth robe.

"Hey, hey, you're not alone," Jeremy consoled her. She could hear in his voice that she'd hurt him. "You've got me, remember? I'm here. I'm always here for you."

"Oh, I know you are, but..." Cathy opened her eyes to find the handsome bath installer standing at the kitchen door, watching the scene. Straightening away from Jeremy, she wiped the tears from her cheeks. "Yes? Is there anything I can do for you?"

She hated herself for being so curt, but Cathy hated crying in front of other people. It was embarrassing. And for him to catch her in Jeremy's arms...

"I'm sorry," the installer said. "I heard crying and..." His thought trailed off as he stared daggers at Jeremy.

Men were so strange.

"Oh," Cathy said. "This is Jeremy, my tenant. He rents the basement suite."

The installer man nodded, then wiped his hand on his overalls and stuck it out for Jeremy to shake. "Vance. Good to meet you."

Vance! Vance rhymes with dance, trance, pants... Vance likes to trance dance in his underpants. Oh, these silly memory aides made Cathy smile—unlike the men, who were still glowering at one another like a pair of apes.

"So, how long is this installation going to take?" Jeremy asked, puffing out his chest like a peacock.

"I'll be done by five," Vance said. "Just like I told your landlord."

Cathy shook her head as the kettle burbled and clicked off behind her. "Anybody care for some tea?"

"Is it going to be noisy?" Jeremy asked, taking one step closer to Vance.

"There will be some noise involved, yes."

"Dust?"

"No, not much dust."

"But noise?"

"Yes, noise."

These men were ridiculous.

"Well, we don't want to keep you from your work," Jeremy said, and then grabbed Cathy's hand. "We'll be in the basement if you need anything. So long."

Cathy caught a glimmer of jealousy in Vance's eyes as Jeremy dragged her down into his suite. She wanted to be upset with him, but she was strangely amused by his guard-dog demeanor.

"Jeremy!" she said, trying not to laugh. "You brat! That man's going to think we're down here doing..."

"Doing what?" Jeremy pulled her into his subterranean bedroom and swept off his robe. He was naked underneath, as usual, and he wrapped his fist around his hard cock, pumping it slowly while she watched. "Doing this?"

Cathy reached out to touch it, and he swept her into a hot kiss. She loved the slick sensation of his precum on her fingers. Making love with a man twenty-five years her junior was like falling into a time warp. She was young every time they fucked. He made her young again.

Releasing their kiss, Jeremy unbuttoned her cardigan and tore it off. "You know what I want?"

Bang, bang, bang! Vance was working away up there, making all the noise he'd promised. Jeremy fought back by turning on his radio. Classic rock. Something they could always agree on.

"You know what I want?" Jeremy asked again.

She grinned while he undid her khakis and pushed them down. "What do you want, Jeremy?"

"This." Thrusting his hand beneath her panties, he cupped her mound and squeezed. "I want your pussy, Cath."

His breath was so hot on her ear she nearly fainted as he tore off her camisole.

"Nobody's ever talked to me the way you do," she told him.

"You're no withering flower," he said, rubbing her clit. "You can take it."

He always did that, always came on too strong. Not the words—Cathy loved his filthy mouth—but the touching.

She pulled back and said, "Lube..."

But Jeremy had a better idea. He tore off her panties and tossed her on the bed like a sack of flour. It made her laugh, the way he manhandled her, because he wouldn't do it if he thought of her as a frail old woman. It was nice to be treated with respect, especially when respect came with a side order of hot sex.

Bowing between her open legs, Jeremy lunged at her pussy, licking her with that warm, wet tongue of his. Her clit throbbed in time with the music on the radio and the hammering upstairs.

Cathy hoped she'd get pounded every bit as hard as that old bathtub!

"What do you want?" Jeremy challenged her. "Tell me or you don't get it."

Cathy loved and hated this game. "I want... oh, it's hard to say."

"No, it's easy." Jeremy petted her thigh with his stubbly cheek. "Go on. Say it."

Lying back on Jeremy's bed, she gazed up at the cheap light fixture she'd picked out years ago. "I want you to lick my clit."

"Lick it?" Jeremy asked. "Is that all? Just lick it?"

"And suck it too."

"Ahh!" Jeremy stretched his big tongue across her pussy and moved in slow circles.

God, that felt good.

So good Cathy couldn't help moaning, even though there was a man just upstairs who might hear. No, he'd never hear, not over the pounding and the music.

Cathy let loose a little as Jeremy licked her clit in long strokes, getting her lips all wet with his saliva. He even stuck his tongue inside her pussy and fucked her with it, which no one had ever done to her before. It was a strange sensation, nothing like a finger or a cock, but she rather liked it.

"Suck now," she said, feeling slightly more comfortable giving orders now that her arousal had been bumped up a few notches. "Suck my clit, Jeremy. Make me come."

"Already?" Jeremy teased. "My landlady is so demanding!"

"Am I?" She grabbed his hair and held him between her legs. "I could demand more."

"I'm sure you will," he said before wrapping his lips around her clit and sucking an orgasm clear out of her body.

It used to take such effort to make her come. Everything was different with Jeremy. His mouth was like magic. He knew just where to lick and just how to suck. Once Jeremy's tongue met her clit, it never took long for that buzzing pleasure in her belly to burst wide open, sending streaks of lightning through her thighs and up into her breasts.

She loved his tongue.

She shouted and shrieked her love of it until he pulled away just to look at her.

"What?" she asked.

He shrugged. "I can't get over how beautiful you are."

Cathy rolled her eyes, but her heart glowed. "Silly."

"No, it's true." He looked at her seriously. "You know it's true. Cathy, you're the most beautiful woman I've ever known."

She believed he believed it. That was enough.

"You know what I want now?" he asked.

She smirked. "You have to tell me or you don't get it."

His eyes blazed as he tore open the sheets. "I want to get under these covers with you and fuck you slow and hard. I want you to feel me inside of you, Cath. I mean, really feel me."

Cathy could scarcely breathe as she pressed her body between the sheets, waiting for Jeremy to follow. For a young man, he knew just what to say to make her throb with want. She maintained a rule that they must each sleep in their own bed at night, but at times like these, that rule seemed really stupid.

At night, she always missed his heat. She missed his body.

But it was here now, settling right on top of her, the heat of his groin meeting the wet fire of hers. He found her pussy with his cock and pressed it slowly inside, small thrusts, working his way in without making her pang. She loved that about him: he'd learned her body like a book. He'd studied it, discovered little nooks she didn't know she had. Jeremy was a better lover than all the rest combined.

Not that there'd been many.

His mouth found her neck, and he kissed her, nipped and bit. His affection made her writhe, driving her pelvis harder against his. He thrust inside her, filling her pussy to the brim.

She could feel his cock throbbing against the walls of her body as he moved in her. He was amazing, and she told him so. She whispered words to him, so many she lost count. Dirty words. Loving words. Everything she thought he'd want to hear, and everything she knew she had to say.

He kissed her lips and she ran her hands down his back, down his ass. She squeezed his firm cheeks, pushing them forward in hopes that he would fuck her harder. When that didn't work, she whispered the word *harder* over and over again.

"Harder?" he asked. "You want it harder?"

"Yes."

He took hold of her wrists and pressed them against the mattress, propping himself up at the same time. Half-kneeling between her open legs, he rutted like an animal, like a bull. She watched as his face turned red, and his neck. The muscles in his arms clenched as he thrust inside of her, hard, just like she wanted. He panted as he fucked her, and she moaned and groaned and howled, praying the music masked her voice.

When she knew he was close, she clamped down on him as hard as she possibly could. He groaned and said her name and every muscle in his body turned to marble. For five seconds, Jeremy was a statue.

When he came out of his orgasm pose, he fell into the cradle of her body and they held each other.

While he slept, she stared at the ceiling.

Had Vance heard them fucking? Was he up there listening through the vents? In a strange, almost embarrassing way, she hoped so. For some reason she couldn't quite elucidate, she wanted that man to know she was a sexual being.

She wasn't dead yet.

ASCENDING THE STAIRCASE an hour later felt quite a lot like a walk of shame.

Cathy allowed Jeremy to take the lead.

"Hey, what are you doing nosing around in our fridge?" Jeremy called out from the top of the stairs.

Vance sounded flustered, saying, "I'm sorry, I just thought I'd grab a glass of water. Cathy offered before..."

"It's okay, Vance! Help yourself to anything you want." Cathy pushed her way in front of Jeremy, hoping to prevent an outbreak of violence between the two men—mostly because she knew very well Jeremy would lose.

"Thank you," Vance said, taking hold of Cathy's hand and squeezing it.

All she could think was that she hadn't washed since she and Jeremy...

"Maybe I could get that cup of coffee now?" Vance asked.

"He's barely been working an hour and already he's taking a break?" Jeremy scoffed.

A surge of anger coursed through Cathy's veins. She wasn't sure why, but she felt it necessary to defend the bath installer.

"Jeremy," Cathy said. "Looks like we've had more snow. Would you get out the shovel and do the driveway, please?"

He stared daggers at her, but eventually suited up in his winter coat and boots and went outside.

"Sorry about that," she said to Vance. "Have a seat. I'll put the coffee on. Would you like some Christmas cookies? I've been baking up a storm for when my mother comes."

All at once, she felt sad.

Vance must have seen it in her body, because he said, "It's going to be quite a transition, isn't it?"

Cathy busied herself with the coffee maker. She didn't want to cry again. "The whole family's coming for Christmas, which is a first in itself. We used to gather at my mother's house, but we sold it when she went into the seniors' home." Cathy always got defensive about that decision. "It was the best place for her, really, after her stroke. There were healthcare workers on staff, people who could really take care of her."

"I'm sure," Vance said, and his voice was so deep and consoling she just wanted to curl up inside it. "Sounds like you care a whole lot about your mother."

That made Cathy feel even more defensive, because she struggled daily with that question. "To tell you the truth, I don't want her living here. It'll be like I'm a teenager all over again. My freedom goes right out the window. What woman my age wants to be accountable to her mother? No one! I don't want this to happen. Every morning, I wake up hoping it's all been a dream."

Gazing out the kitchen window, Cathy watched Jeremy working away at the thick blanket of snow coating her driveway. What the hell was she going to do about him? How could she possibly hide their relationship from her family if her mother was living under the same roof? Sure her hearing wasn't the best, but the woman wasn't stupid. She'd catch on.

"You said your mother had a stroke?" Vance asked. "How is her recovery going?"

"Oh." Cathy had nearly forgotten he was in the room. She grabbed a container full of sugar cookies and joined him at the table. "She's actually doing amazingly well. It was terrible, when it first happened. We wondered if she'd ever be able to communicate again, but she worked with this incredible music therapist at the home and little by little the speech came back. It's been nothing short of a miracle."

"So the home was the right choice at the time, sounds like."

Cathy smiled at the recognition that she and her siblings had made a good decision. "I truly believe that it was."

"And her living with you is the best choice at this stage?"

The kitchen filled with the dark aroma of fresh-brewed coffee as Cathy mulled over that question. "You know, it really is the best thing for her and the family. My sister's still got kids at home, my one brother lives in Japan, and my other brother has his own problems to deal with. Me, I've got the space, so..." Cathy shrugged. "Here we are."

"Here we are." With an encouraging smile, Vance picked up a cookie dusted with sparkling red and green sugar. It was an amusing image, watching this muscle-bound fix-it man nibbling away at her dainty little cookies. She couldn't help picturing what he'd look like nibbling at other sweet things.

They chatted about family over a coffee break that stretched on and on. Every time Cathy got the sense Vance might go back to work, she'd ask him another question to keep him in the room. He was just so easy to talk to, and he had so many interesting stories about other seniors he'd installed special tubs for over the years. If he saw that they might need a hand with errands or tasks around the house, he offered to come back another day just to help them out.

Vance was like a one-man community service provider.

"Does your wife mind that you spend all your spare time helping out strangers instead of being at home with her?" Cathy asked. Vance hadn't mentioned a wife and he wasn't wearing a ring, but she knew that a lot of men in the trades didn't wear them at work because jewellery could be hazardous. She just wanted to know for sure.

Vance seemed to blush as he said, "There's no wife in the picture."

That question must have scared him off, because he stood from the table and said he really should get back to work.

Perfect timing.

Just as Vance's power tools buzzed into action, Jeremy came in from the cold. Cathy comforted him with coffee and cookies, but every time Vance made even the slightest sound, Jeremy furrowed his brow and grumbled about the noise.

Truth be told, the buzzing and hammering was getting to Cathy as well. What a headache!

"I have an idea," she told Jeremy. "Why don't you see if there's anything you can help Vance with while I'm gone?"

"While you're gone?" Jeremy set his coffee mug down with a thud. "Where are you going?"

Away from this racket!

"Oh, I've got a little more Christmas shopping to do before the family gets here. You think you can hold down the fort?"

Jeremy half-grimaced, half-smirked. Cathy knew how much he enjoyed playing man of the house. As much as she wanted to stick around and watch Vance work, she knew her ogling would upset Jeremy as much as the construction noise was hurting her brain.

Wishing the boys a fond farewell, she set off for the relative peace of a shopping mall in December.

SEXY SURPRISES FOR CHRISTMAS

WHEN CATHY RETURNED home, Vance's van was still parked outside.

The house was quiet when she opened the door, except for the whispered voices of two men she quite liked. Setting her bags by the door, she made her way to the bathroom. She was shocked to find Vance and Jeremy actually... smiling!

Laughing, chatting, working together.

"My goodness!" Cathy said. "Would you look at this?"

She meant the men, but they obviously thought she was talking about the bathtub.

"Yup," Vance said. "Just a few finishing touches and it'll be ready for a test drive."

Cathy tried not to flirt with him in front of Jeremy, but she couldn't contain herself. "Who's going to get naked, hmm Vance? Is that part of your job description?"

Jeremy surprised her by saying, "I think we all should."

Cathy waited for Vance to sneer at the idea, but he only shot Jeremy a non-committal grin.

"Looks just like it did in the brochure," Cathy said, because the men's silence was making her nervous. "My mother will be so pleased."

"We were talking a lot about her when you were gone," Jeremy said. "And about you, too."

"Oh." Cathy glanced between them. "You were?"

Vance was standing inside the bathtub, securing the door. He gave Jeremy a look Cathy didn't understand, and then asked, "Do you want me to leave the room?"

"No, no. This was your idea." Jeremy took something out of his pocket and held it between his hands. As Vance looked on, he said, "Cathy, I've been trying to give you the same Christmas present for the past three years. It's wrapped and ready to go. Then at the last minute I chicken out, every time. Vance and I got to talking, and I think the time is right for me to stop being a chicken and finally give you this gift."

Getting down on one knee on the bathroom tile, Jeremy opened his hands to reveal a box, and then opened the box to reveal a ring. "Cathy, we've lived together for years and I can't imagine living without you. Will you marry me?"

Cathy laughed. This had to be a dream. Had to be! What kind of attractive young man would want to hitch his wagon to a silly old woman and her elderly mother?

But Jeremy wasn't laughing, and Vance actually looked hurt by her reaction.

"You're serious, Jeremy? This is really what you want?"

His shoulders fell and he looked down at his ring. "Not if you don't. I mean, I want to marry you, but you obviously don't feel the same way, so never mind."

"No, no Jeremy." Cathy sat on the closed lid of the toilet to be closer to him. "I just thought you couldn't be serious, with my mother moving in and... well, I'm so much older than you. Are you sure about this? You can do so much better."

"Better?" he scoffed. "What makes a good marriage? Love, respect, and compatibility. What do we have? Love, respect, and compatibility."

"And great sex, from what I hear," Vance added.

Cathy felt a blush coming on. Too many thoughts ran through her mind all at once. The big one was: *what will my mother say?* But, for goodness' sake, she couldn't let her mother determine her happiness!

"Yes," Cathy said. "The answer is yes. There's a lot to sort out, but we'll do it together. I want to be married to you, Jeremy. I love you more than life."

Pulling her to standing, he slid the engagement ring onto her finger. It looked antique, but the fit was perfect. Everything about this moment was perfect—even the fact that they were standing in the bathroom with Vance applauding from inside the tub.

"Vance and I were talking about something else, too," Jeremy said. When he started unbuttoning his plaid shirt, Cathy wondered if this really was a dream. "Since these are some of your last days living in your house without your mother, we thought you deserved something really special."

"Something unforgettable," Vance agreed. He shifted his tools out of the tub. "Jeremy says you've got a fantasy about being with two men at once."

Cathy swatted Jeremy's now-naked chest. "You brat! How could you say that to a stranger?"

"The funny thing is, Cathy, you don't feel like a stranger to me." Vance unbuckled his overalls, one clip and then the other, but he didn't let go of the straps. "I feel like I've known you all my life."

"I know what you mean," she admitted. "I feel the same way about you, to be honest. I don't know what it is."

Vance dropped his pants and tore off his top. Nothing left but tightie-whities that admirably showed off his bulge. His bare chest looked exactly the way she'd imagined it: expansive, muscular, a prairie of blond fuzz sprouting across it. His nipples were so hard and so pink she wanted to lick them, but she looked to Jeremy first, amazed that he seemed okay with this.

41

"Merry Christmas, Cathy." Jeremy dropped his pants and stepped inside the newly installed shower tub. "Come on and test this out with us."

Two men in underpants beckoning her into a state-of-the-art shower-bath? This was like the twilight zone!

"It's quite spacious, isn't it?" Cathy said, trying not to stare at the men's significant bulges.

"The seat here flips down when you're using it and up when you're not." When Vance displayed the action, Cathy took that opportunity to gaze at the thick outline of his cock beneath stretchy white fabric. Her legs nearly gave out on her.

"Get in here so Vance can turn the water on," Jeremy said. "What's wrong, afraid to get your feet wet?"

Cathy bit her lip, still trying not to look directly at the men's nearly naked bodies. She focused her attention on the tub itself, which was beige and chest-high, with a water-tight door to get in and out. It was tall rather than long, more like a shower stall you could sit in.

"Hurry up or we're starting without you," Jeremy teased.

Raising her brow, Cathy said, "Now *that* I wouldn't mind seeing."

Vance laughed, and no sooner took off his underwear.

This time, Cathy couldn't help staring. His cock was just getting hard, still half-sitting on the pillow of his balls. When he took it in his hand and started stroking, Cathy just about fainted.

"What about you, Jeremy?" Cathy closed the bathroom door before stripping down to her bra and panties. "Aren't you going to get naked for me?"

"I can't compete with that thing," he laughed, but took off his undies anyway.

Like a zombie woman hungry for cock, Cathy stepped over Vance's tools. As he showed her how to secure the door so it wouldn't leak, Jeremy unclasped her bra and pulled down her panties.

She told herself this was a dream. It couldn't possibly be real. And if it wasn't real... well, she wasn't going to worry about propriety any longer.

Vance turned on the shower to wash any stray dirt and dust down the drain, and she jumped at him.

"Is this okay, Jeremy?" Cathy asked, but she didn't wait for his answer before kissing Vance.

His mouth was powerful, hungry, everything she'd expected it to be. Jeremy was an excellent kisser, but he was sweet compared to this. Vance was a tiger, rough and hot. He growled as he kissed her, still working his cock in his huge calloused hand. Cathy took over. Her hands weren't big or hard, but who knows? Maybe he'd appreciate her tender approach.

"We made a decision while you were gone." It was Jeremy's voice, behind her.

She broke away from Vance's mouth, only for a moment. "What's did you decide?"

Vance took the opportunity to plug the drain, and switch the flow from shower to bath. Water started filling up around their naked feet. "We decided to take you the way you've always dreamed of. I'll fuck your pussy."

"And I'll fuck your ass," Jeremy said.

Cathy swallowed hard through the rising steam. "At the same time, you mean?"

Jeremy slapped her ass crack with lube. "It's what you've always wanted."

That was true. She'd dreamed of double penetration for years, but she never thought it would become a reality. Two men at once? These things didn't happen in real life. Certainly not in Cathy's life.

And yet here they were, Vance and Jeremy, both ready and willing and naked in her shower.

"Okay," Cathy said. "Where do we start?"

"We start here." Jeremy thrust his erection up and down her ass crack, slathering lube all around her eager hole. "Maybe Vance can suck your tits while I get a head start."

"Oh my God!"

Vance reset the bath seat and plunked his muscular ass down on it. He reminded her of a Rodin bronze, such a strong and forceful image. When he pulled her into his arms, she brought Jeremy along as well. The water had almost risen to their ankles. Her skin started to tingle.

"Yes, please," Cathy begged as she watched Vance's mouth approaching her nipple.

His features were chiselled like a rock face, firm planes, square jaw. His tongue was something else altogether: warm, wet, giving. When he sucked her nipple, she'd have fallen over if Jeremy wasn't holding her up from behind.

But he wanted his turn too, of course. While Vance licked and sucked her tits, Jeremy pressed his slick mushroom head to Cathy's asshole. She loved anal, but they did it rarely enough that it was still a treat. She knew she had to breathe with him, but it was hard to stay relaxed with Vance's mouth wrapped around her nipple.

"Oh God, that feels so good!"

"What does?" Jeremy asked. His voice was like gravel.

"Everything." She focused on her tight ass ring, willing it to go slack so Jeremy's cock could come inside. Easier said than done. It was such a squeeze, fitting his dick in there.

So instead, she focused on the warm water caressing her feet while Vance's tongue lashed her nipples. She arched toward his face, feeding him more of her breast. Her back curved, sending her butt skyward, and Jeremy splayed open her cheeks as he pushed himself inside.

"Oh God!" Cathy cried as Jeremy's tip plunged inside her ass. It hurt like hell, but not in a bad way—in a way that was impossible to explain.

"Keep going?" he asked.

"Oh yes," she said. "Oh yes."

He pushed his cock in slowly, easing a pathway. The lube helped vastly. Lube was a godsend, and usually a necessity for her pussy too, but she was amazed to feel a slickness between her thighs. The two men working her over had generated an incredible amount of juice.

Now she was ready for anything.

Or so she thought.

WHEN JEREMY LAUNCHED his cock fully inside her hole, stretching her ass to its limits, Vance stood in front of her. He growled like an animal as he looked over Cathy's naked body.

She felt like a rabbit with nowhere to run.

And she liked it.

"Yes," she said, nodding deeply. "Do it."

A wily smirk grew across his lips.

Vance surprised Cathy by grabbing her thighs and lifting her clear out of the mounting water. She struggled for the seat Vance had abandoned, setting both feet on top of it, on either side of Vance's tremendous body. Jeremy groaned all the while, no doubt because her ass muscles clamped his cock every time she moved.

She was all theirs, held aloft by Vance in front and Jeremy at the rear.

Never in her life had she felt so vulnerable and so aroused simultaneously.

Her legs were splayed, her hands clinging to Vance's thick neck. He was a hell of a man. Thank goodness Jeremy was open to fulfilling this fantasy with her. The kind of man who would share the woman he loved if that's what she wanted? Well, that kind of man was a keeper.

"God, your pussy." Vance shook his head as he stared between her legs.

"What's it doing?" she asked.

Jeremy laughed and his erection throbbed inside her ass. The burn was turning into a pleasant glow, not so painful anymore.

"It's wet," Vance answered. "It's wet and pink and wonderful."

Cathy felt a blush coming on. "Well, I think you have something to do with its state of arousal—both of you." She tried to turn and look at Jeremy, but she was locked between the men. "I can't believe this is really happening."

"Believe it," Vance said, pressing his cockhead at the mouth of her pussy.

The water had risen almost to the men's knees, and it sloshed around in the tub as Vance forced himself inside of her.

The sensation was like nothing she'd ever experienced. With Jeremy's cock already filling her ass, her pussy had next to no room for Vance.

That didn't stop him, of course. He rammed his thick erection into her pussy so hard she felt it all the way up her spine.

"It hurts!" she said.

"I'm sorry." Vance started pulling out, but Cathy clamped down on him as hard as she could.

"No, stay." Cathy wasn't finished with him yet, hurt or no hurt. "Please, I need this."

"Are you sure?"

"Yes!" Cathy tried to buck forward to show him how much she wanted it, but she really couldn't move. Pressing her heels down on the bath seat, she attempted to rock between them, but even that didn't work. She was totally at their mercy.

Closing her eyes, Cathy clung to Vance's neck while her back side settled into Jeremy's chest. The water level was rising. She could feel the odd splash against her ass. They had to hurry before the tub overflowed.

"Is this okay?" Vance asked as his cock surged inside her.

"Yes," she said. "It's perfect. Don't stop."

Was she crazy, or could she feel the men's hard cocks rubbing against each other? They were separated only by a thin membrane.

The thought of Vance and Jeremy's erections so close to one another, almost touching, made her moan, and the men seemed revved up by that reaction. They moved faster inside of her, Vance thrusting forward while Jeremy leaned back. The music of their motion echoed in the water, which splashed around their legs, dancing again Cathy's bum. It tickled at first, licking her skin like a warm tongue, then rising to coat her flesh.

She trembled in their arms. Her nipples had gone so hard they actually hurt. She wanted to move, but couldn't. Only Vance and Jeremy could move, driving their throbbing cocks in and out. She could have sworn she felt their engorged tips pressing one against the other.

The bliss of pain and pleasure transported her to a place she'd never been. Vance kissed her hard, thumbing her nipple. Oh yes. Oh yes, yes, yes! She was coming before she knew it, crying out as the bathwater flirted with her hips.

The men worked her hard, grunting and groaning as she floated between them.

Who would come first?

She clamped her muscles down on their cocks, and Jeremy's reaction was huge. He bucked deep inside her ass, just one thrust and then a tortured groan, like a wounded animal.

With Jeremy's cock stationary in Cathy's ass, Vance worked ever harder, driving his dick into the depths of her pussy over and over again.

"This is it," Vance moaned. "Oh, I'm gonna come. I'm gonna come so hard!"

His firm jaw clenched and his eyes squeezed shut. His face went beet red as he lodged himself in her pussy. He'd found ecstasy in Cathy's body, and she couldn't be more proud.

WHEN THE MEN EASED themselves out of Cathy's orgasm-weary body, her two holes ached.

She wasn't sure if she felt relieved, or if she missed them.

The water had risen high in the tub, just short of spilling over the sides.

Cathy let her arms float as Vance turned off the water.

"So, what do you think?" he asked.

"Of the tub or the sex?" she teased. "No, the tub is very nice. I'm sure my mother will be pleased."

Jeremy must have seen her thoughts, because he took her in his arms and held her tight. Their naked bodies slid one against the other, and she thought how much she'd miss their freedom once Christmas arrived and her mother came to stay.

There was something infinitely sad about a last hoorah.

"Some way to celebrate an engagement, huh?" Jeremy asked. "A threesome with a guy we just met."

"Engagement…" Christ, Cathy had forgotten about that already. "My God, we're engaged. Oh, that's going to go down a treat with Mom. She'll probably think I'm your sugar mama."

Vance joined in their embrace, hugging Cathy from behind. It felt wonderful to be so protected. The men created a cocoon all around her, and the lovely bathwater filled the gaps with velvety warmth.

"It's sure to take some adjustment," Vance said. "But it's better for you and Jeremy to face the hurdles together instead of pretending your love doesn't exist."

"See?" Jeremy said. "This guy knows what he's talking about."

Cathy laughed, because these men sure were singing a different tune earlier in the day.

"Look, I've got plenty of experience working with elderly clients," Vance said, hugging Cathy so close she could feel his spent cock against her backside. "Any problems, any challenges, any help you need, I'm only a phone call away. I'm serious."

"I know you are." Cathy choked back tears. She'd never felt so cared for, and by two wonderful men with so much to offer. "I never thought I'd be so lucky. What a gift."

"Nothing you don't deserve," Jeremy said, and kissed her forehead while Vance kissed her hair. "You've got a good heart, Cath. Thanks for sharing it."

The countdown had begun. Christmas was closing in, but that thought no longer caused Cathy pain. Jeremy was right: she had a big enough heart to share her home with family, friends, bathtub installers, and especially her wonderful fiancée.

Stranded with the Professor

"D inner couldn't have been lovelier, Rosa." Professor Klein patted his moustache with his napkin, and then stood from the table. "Unfortunately, I must be off. Long drive ahead. Jacob, would you like a ride home?"

"Huh? What'd I do?" Jacob looked up from his second helping of pumpkin pie. He hadn't exactly been following the conversation. His parents' friends were so boring he'd tuned them out all through Christmas dinner.

"Professor Klein offered you a ride," Jacob's mother said, shooting him an incomprehensible glare. "Why don't you go with him, dear? Better than catching the bus, don't you think?"

Why head back to campus Christmas night? Jacob had planned on staying at least another day or two. Hell, he still had laundry in the dryer. Oh great, now his father was glaring at him too.

"I have to go already?" Jacob asked. He didn't want to be rude, but he'd been looking forward to a couple more lazy days in his old bedroom.

His mother nodded. "Come, let's fold your laundry while your father packs your gifts into the professor's car."

"Mom, what's going on?" Jacob asked as he followed her down the basement stairs. "Why do I have to go back tonight?"

His mother pulled clean sheets from the dryer, rolled them into a clumsy ball, and tossed them in his laundry bag. "Might as well hitch a ride." She was avoiding Jacob's gaze, which she only did when she was lying.

"What's the real reason, Mom?"

She sighed and shook her head. "You didn't hear a word that man said, did you? The professor's had a rough December. His *man-friend* left him, just three weeks before Christmas. Can you imagine? Oh, and they'd been together almost fifteen years. I don't want him driving home alone."

"Why? What's he gonna do, drive into a tree? He's a grown man. He'll be fine."

Jacob watched his mother ball up his clothes and toss them into the laundry bag. That was some angry clothes-balling, and he couldn't blame her. It was compassionate of his parents to take in anyone spending Christmas alone. They were good people. Why was he being a dick and thinking only of himself?

Why?

Because, though he didn't like to admit it, gay men made Jacob uncomfortable.

He wasn't homophobic. Honestly, he wasn't. The problem was more that... well, Jacob didn't like to admit this either, but every time he found himself alone with a gay guy, he got this overwhelming urge to pounce. If he did, he'd be gay too. Was he really ready for that kind of commitment?

"Fine, I'll go." Jacob closed the dryer as his grinning mother tied up his laundry bag.

"That's my good boy," his mother said, handing it to him.

Jacob's heart beat a little faster as they climbed the stairs. If he didn't know better, he'd think he was excited.

Professor Klein's car was nicer than Jacob expected. It had heated leather seats, which was an undeniable perk on a cold December night.

"This is a lot nicer than the bus," Jacob said. They'd been on the road for almost ten minutes and the professor hadn't spoken at all. The silence made him nervous.

Professor Klein seemed beyond distracted. "Hmm? Oh, yes. Thank you."

If only it were light outside so Jacob could start reading for next term. Professor Klein obviously wasn't interested in talking to him. Even though Jacob attended the same university the professor taught at, their paths never crossed. They weren't in the same department. Come to think of it, Jacob couldn't remember which department he worked in.

The drive back to campus took almost two hours at the best of times. With tonight's flurries, it could take up to three. Might as well make conversation.

"So, what do you teach?" Jacob asked.

"Sociolinguistics."

"Oh." Jacob gazed past his reflection in the darkened window. Sure was getting snowy out there. "I don't know what that is."

"Linguistic variation and its social significance," the professor replied. "Next term I'm guiding courses in language acquisition, language and ethnicity, as well as a second-year general sociolinguistics class."

That probably would have been interesting to someone who knew what the professor was talking about. "I'm a math geek," Jacob admitted. "So I'm all about numbers. Words aren't exactly my... thing."

"Ahh."

This was hopeless. When the professor turned on the radio and tuned in to a classical station, Jacob set his head against the window and closed his eyes. Maybe it was rude of him, maybe his mother wouldn't approve, but the turkey and red wine with dinner had made him sleepy. He drifted off, and when he awoke forty-five minutes had gone by.

And the car wasn't moving.

"Huh?" Jacob jerked upright in his seat and wiped the drool from his chin. "What happened?"

"A blizzard, looks like." Professor Klein leaned forward to fiddle with the radio dial. His station was fuzzy, and he settled, with a sigh, on classic rock. "Hopefully it lets up soon, but it's coming down like a blanket just now. We kept passing other cars that had pulled off the road, so I thought it best to follow suit."

Jacob peered out the window. All he saw was white. And then, of course, he had to pee. "Shit."

"In a hurry to get back to campus?" the professor asked.

"No, it's not that. Just gotta write my name in the snow." Jacob opened the car door and was amazed to find himself in a winter wonderland. Snow tumbled down like cotton balls, but in such volume it obscured the road and everything on it. Any smart driver would have pulled over, like Professor Klein had done.

Jacob ambled through the heavy carpet of snow. He spotted a ditch that way and he didn't want to fall in a pit, so he peed from there. The air wasn't super-cold, thank goodness.

It wasn't until he was half done that Jacob realized the professor might be watching. The idea of being watched felt strangely exciting. Could Professor Klein see Jacob's dick? Did the mustache man want it in his mouth? What would it feel like to get sucked off by a guy with facial hair?

Jacob shivered with the thrill of that idea. As he zipped up, all he could imagine was the professor's head bobbing against his pelvis, looking down to see the streaks of grey in the older man's tawny hair. Or his eyes—what colour were the professor's eyes?

When Jacob opened his door, Professor Klein sat upright, sniffling. He shoved a hanky into his jacket pocket. His eyes were puffy and red. Was he... was he *crying*?

"Hey," Jacob said as he got in the car. "You okay, man?"

The professor gazed down at Jacob's high tops. "Your shoes are wet now. And your pants! Are you trying to get frostbite, or are you just abominably stupid?"

Geeze! Didn't this guy realize Jacob was doing him a favour by riding shotgun? Did he have to be so rude? Jacob tried not to respond in kind, but he found himself saying, "Why are you being such a dick? The heater can dry my shoes. Fuck! I'm not an idiot."

"The heater won't be on for long. If I don't turn the engine off soon, we'll burn off every bit of gas in the tank, and when the storm finally clears we'll be stuck out here."

Jacob hadn't considered that the blizzard might last longer than a couple minutes, but the professor's warning reminded him of something he'd heard on the news last winter: an entire highway in Quebec was closed down for a matter of days by a blizzard so dense even emergency vehicles couldn't make it through. Hadn't people died in their cars? Jacob thought he remembered hearing that a few drivers had frozen to death.

"Maybe we should try driving some more," Jacob suggested. "How far are we from the nearest town?"

"I haven't the faintest idea. I couldn't see road signs. That's part of the reason I pulled over. I couldn't see a thing."

Jacob took off his shoes and pressed his feet to the heating vents.

"Thank you," the professor said. "That's lovely."

"I want to dry my socks before we turn off the car."

The professor sighed. "Very well. That's probably a smart idea."

Finally Jacob wasn't being called an idiot. He smiled smugly, and then felt guilty, though her wasn't sure why. "We're in for a long night, huh?"

"It would seem so."

For a couple minutes, they said nothing. It felt like hours had gone by when Jacob asked, "Were you crying before?"

No response.

"You can tell me about it if you want, Professor Klein."

"Please, call me Max."

"Is that your name?" *Stupid, stupid, stupid!*

Professor Klein laughed. "Yes, my name is Max."

"I like that name." Jacob was flirting. He knew it and he couldn't stop and he didn't want to. "My mom said you had a rough break-up. Sorry about that. If there's anything I can do..."

"I'm not the sort to talk about these things." Max had been staring at the dashboard, but he looked into Jacob's face in that moment. He had hazel eyes flecked with gold. Now Jacob knew.

"I thought you were a psycholinguistics guy," Jacob said, trying to raise Max's spirits. "Doesn't that mean you're, like, introspective and talky and stuff?"

Max smiled sadly. "*Sociolinguistics*, not psycholinguistics, and it means I study why people say things like 'like' and 'stuff'."

It took a moment for Jacob to figure out what the guy was talking about. He wasn't getting anywhere poking and prodding about this break-up. Now the professor liked him even less than before.

"Looong night ahead." Jacob gazed at his reflection in the window. Not a single car had passed them on this back road. Outside, it was getting super-snowy and blustery too. Conditions were worsening.

"After we turn off the engine, I suggest we huddle together for warmth," the professor said, matter-of-factly, like there was no erotic potential in that statement. "Your gifts are in the trunk, but if we shuffle them to the front seats we can fold down the back ones and get some sleep."

Jacob's breath caught in his throat. "Sounds like you've done this before."

"Thankfully no." Max was already halfway out the door. "Mental preparedness is key. We can use your laundry as insulation."

"Okay..."

"Are your feet dry?"

"Yeah..."

"Good." With that, Professor Klein turned the key in the ignition and the night closed in on them. Darkness and snow. Nothing to hear but breathing and heartbeats.

Since he wasn't wearing shoes, Jacob climbed through the space between the two front seats and fell into the makeshift bed Max had prepared for them. He'd put a fitted sheet around the horizontal back seats and piled socks, underwear, t-shirts, sweaters and everything else on top. It was strangely comforting to cuddle up in clean laundry.

Max crawled in back and closed the car door. His motions were decided and sure, like there was no deeper meaning to the night's events.

"Do we... keep our clothes on, or what?" Jacob asked. He knew which answer he was hoping for, even if it scared the bejesus out of him. "For heat, I mean."

The night was dark and light at once. The snow shone so brightly it actually became a light source. Max stared past Jacob and into the blizzard. He said the words *clothes off* with such certainty Jacob believed that was the thing to do.

They undressed quickly in the confined space. Completely naked, Jacob buried himself in laundry, which was, amazingly, still warm from the dryer. Max was somewhere behind him, but not touching him. The professor stretched a sheet and then a blanket over their bodies and the laundry pile. Jacob felt the warmth trapped next to his skin even as the coldness of night encroached.

"Closer," Jacob said.

For the longest moment in the history of everything, Max didn't move.

And then he did.

"You won't tell your parents...?"

Jacob smiled. "I won't tell them if you don't tell them... whatever happens."

Max drew in closer. His body heat met Jacob's back, and then his skin did too. Chest to back, arms circling around, hard cock lodged between two very receptive ass cheeks.

Yes, thank you!

Jacob couldn't get over the mass of that erection, or the heat coming off it. The professor's arousal encouraged his erection to

58

swell. He ached to touch it, but he was frozen in place. Couldn't move a muscle.

"If I've been rude to you, I apologize." Max hugged Jacob hard, then planted a hot kiss at the crook of his neck. That mustache tickled, but Jacob didn't laugh. "I'm not the type to talk about my emotions, but I appreciate your compassion—more than you'll ever know."

Jacob warmed from the inside out. "You can do anything you want to me. I mean it. Anything."

A growl emerged from deep in Max's throat. He sieged Jacob's neck with kisses, sweeping his mustache up its length and down Jacob's shoulder. Was this really happening? Was Jacob about to lose his butt-cherry to a professor from his very own school?

A hot hand met Jacob's dick, and he gasped. He seriously couldn't believe how good it felt. Nothing like touching himself. Nothing like the rare occasions on which he'd been able to convince a girl to touch it. Max's hand was practiced and sure. It wrapped around Jacob's erection. It tightened, tightened, stroked. If he wasn't careful he'd come before anything really happened.

"Feels good." Jacob's throat clicked between words. "So good."

Max didn't say anything. His staggered breath on Jacob's shoulder said more than words ever could. Jacob wondered if he should reach back and paw at the professor, but he felt nervous about it. He didn't know what he was doing, so he just let Max do all the heavy lifting.

The professor's hand streaked up and down Jacob's erection, and the rampant friction warmed his thighs and his belly. If the plan was to generate heat, it was sure as hell working!

"Reach under the front seat," Max said, loosening his grip on Jacob's shaft. "There's a road safety kit. Flashlights and so forth."

Jacob reached tentatively, like he was afraid something would bite him. He found a plastic box under the seat and pulled it out, unsnapped the clips, opened the lid. "Condoms?" They were right on top.

"And lubrication," Max explained. "Mental preparedness is best followed by physical preparedness."

"Okay." Jacob's head was spinning. He handed the lube and condoms to Max, turning only briefly to catch the wolfish gleam in the professor's eyes. "Does this mean you want to…?"

Max raised an eyebrow, but didn't say anything. He really wasn't much of a talker, was he?

"You want to fuck me?" Jacob asked, swallowing past the lump in his throat.

Max nipped Jacob's shoulder, then kissed the bite better. "Is that what you want?"

"Yes." Jacob's heart thundered in his ears. "Please."

He closed his eyes and listened while Max tore open a condom packet. The shuffling under their makeshift covers made him shiver because it allowed cooler air against his skin. But not for long. Max suited up quickly, then squirted a generous dollop of lube against Jacob's asshole.

"Ohh, that's cold!" He laughed. "I wasn't expecting that."

Max chuckled along, even as he urged one slick finger inside Jacob's ass. "My word, that's a tight squeeze." He whacked Jacob's ass cheek with his sheathed cock. "I'm not sure I'll be able to get this inside. It'll be quite the task, I must say."

Jacob clenched his teeth and his ass in unison. "It'll be fine," he said, more to reassure himself than Max. "I really want it. Really bad."

More lube, and Max impressed another finger upon Jacob's tight hole. "You need to loosen up," Max said. "Relax."

Max reached around Jacob's body and took hold of his cock, clasping it hard, stroking it roughly. Jacob would not last long. Not long at all. But the sweet rubbing helped him relax, just like Max said. He closed his eyes and whined when Max slipped two fingers out and then pressed a slick cockhead against his hole. The ring of muscle reacted violently, closing up tight, saying no to the intruder.

Brushing his mustache the length of Jacob's neck, Max said, "Open up. Let me in."

The professor pressed his thumb to Jacob's seeping cockhead, tracing a pool of precum around it in sensuous circles. Jacob bucked into Max's hand, whispering, "Holy fuck, that's good."

Before Jacob knew it, his asshole responded to the kissing and touching and incredible stroking. Max pushed inside, opening Jacob's hole wider than it had ever been and lodging just the tip of his cock inside.

Jacob whimpered. He couldn't help it. The strain shot through him like lightning, hitting every point from his toes to his nose. When he closed his eyes, he saw stars. Max's tip held his ass ring open, stretching him wide, too wide. Just when he was about to tell the professor to pull out, Max did the opposite: he pushed in, pushed hard until his mushroom tip opened Jacob excruciatingly wide.

Jacob jerked forward. Max held his cock tight, keeping him in place. "Don't fight it. Don't struggle."

He knew Max was right: work through the pain. It would subside if he let go.

"Don't fight it," Max repeated, shuttling his hand up and down Jacob's throbbing erection. He kissed Jacob's neck, bit it. "Come for me."

The professor's cock pulsed in Jacob's ass. It felt huge in there, hot and hard, like it was ready to explode. Jacob knew that feeling all too well. Despite the sizzle and pang of Max's cock in his ass, his impending orgasm felt as close as Max's fist. He started thrusting, driving his erection into the professor's slick grip. Despite the lingering pain, this combination of fucking and stroking felt better than anything he'd ever experienced.

"Come," Max encouraged.

Jacob couldn't hold back any longer. He drove his dick hard enough forward that the professor's hand slipped all the way down to his balls as he blew his load. Jacob came so hard it hurt. He could feel it in his balls, feel his cream's starting point, feel it shoot through his shaft and out his piss slit. It kept coming and coming, like a waterfall, soiling laundry that had been clean only moments ago.

His dick was always super-sensitive after orgasm, so he flicked Max's hand away. No problem for the professor—he had other work to do.

Moving in Jacob's tight ass, Max built up friction as he increased in speed. There was cum on his hand, where he held Jacob's hip. It was slick and still hot. He hooked his chin around Jacob's shoulder, thrusting more decidedly in his ass, making a sure impression.

"It's your turn to come," Jacob said. His voice was unsurprisingly hoarse. "Come in my ass. Please."

Max made a sound that was half chuckle, half groan. He worked over Jacob's ass, thrusting in double time, fucking him relentlessly until all Jacob could feel was friction.

"Oh God," Max chanted, over and over again.

"You're gonna come?"

"Yes. Oh God!"

Max gripped Jacob's hip and slammed his pelvis against Jacob's ass. He was in so deep Jacob would have rolled away if there'd been any chance of escape. As it was, he had to take the pummelling as it came in hot and hard. Max slammed him, rammed him, bullied his ass into submission. How could that huge hard-on open him up so wide? How could he stand being driven so violently? Was Max mad at him, or was this just the way it went with hot man-on-man action?

Filling his ass one last time, Max breathed hard in Jacob's ear. Hot breaths, blazing like the sun. In time, those breaths turned into words. "Thank you."

It was hot under the covers. The windows were all steamed up. Would it get cold before morning? Before the snowfall subsided and the roads were cleared? And would Jacob and Max continue seeing each other on the down low even after they'd returned to campus?

Jacob wouldn't know the answers to those questions until the light of day shone through the snow. For now, he was satisfied by the possibility.

SM, or How I Met My Girlfriend in a Queer Theatre

I figured she'd hate drag queens.

In university, I read a few feminist-lesbian papers that were pretty anti-drag. I can't remember the reasoning. Something about drag performances being reductive and misogynistic, maybe?

Trans women didn't seem to like drag queens much, either. I didn't read that anywhere. It was just my impression from chatting with other queer people. So that's another reason I figured Lisa wouldn't be impressed by the drag show at *Sisters in Sin* Queer Theatre.

By training and profession, Lisa was a stage manager. People were always asking if she aspired to be an actor. She didn't. Lisa liked the backstage bit, every aspect of it, from lighting to sound to last-minute prop repairs. That's one reason she enjoyed working at *Sisters*: in such a tiny theatre, one person did everything, all the backstage stuff. In a big theatre, you'd have had at least one person on lights, someone else doing the sound, even dressers and props managers. Lisa liked to do it all herself.

When I started volunteering at *Sisters in Sin*, a lot of people asked me that same question about wanting to be an actor. In truth, I only started there to meet other queer people. It's hard, when you're not a bar person. Or a club person. I always felt weird just going up to a stranger and talking to them for no reason. I'm a quiet queer. I volunteered to hand out programs at *Sisters* because it seemed like easy work, not too much patron interaction. Quiet queer work.

The first time I saw Lisa, my knees buckled so hard I almost fell into a gay man's lap. She whipped from the backstage area, through the audience, and disappeared into her dark glass booth at the back of the house. It didn't matter that Lisa dressed all in black, or that she moved like a shadow. I spotted her: tall and curvaceous, a full round face, blonde hair pulled into a neat ponytail. She took my breath away.

"You know that's a tranny, right?" another program hander-outer said to me.

My heart nearly stopped. *That word!* I hated that word, and I hated even more that another volunteer, an out loud and proud lesbian, would speak with such ire about a fellow queer. I didn't know what to say, so I played dumb and asked, "Who?"

"The SM," said the other volunteer.

"SM?" I figured that must either be an insult I'd never heard, or the big blond was into sadomasochism.

"Stage Manager," the volunteer clarified.

"Oh." I felt stupid for not knowing, but just because I was volunteering in a theatre didn't mean I knew anything about the different jobs there.

I wanted her name. She was so stunning, even dressed in simple black slacks and a turtleneck. Nothing fancy, except her black velvet scrunchie. I wanted to know everything about her, but I didn't want to hear it from the mean dyke across the aisle.

In truth, I don't remember how I learned Lisa's name. I must have overheard somebody calling her before a show, or afterwards when I stuck around to tidy the theatre.

Like I said, I was always a quiet queer. It took a few weeks of watching and waiting before I finally worked up the courage to talk to her. To *Lisa*. I asked her something sensible. I asked, "Can I help you with anything?"

She was on stage at the time. It wasn't a big stage and it wasn't raised too high. Still, Lisa didn't react. She had this look on her face like she was concentrating hard, and I wondered if she didn't want to be interrupted or if she hadn't heard me.

"Can I help you?" I asked again.

Lisa jumped, like she hadn't realized anybody else was in the theatre. Her shock made me smile. It was such an intense emotion that it sharpened her features, and when she looked at me, the glowing blue of her eyes pierced my very soul. I know that sounds corny, but it's absolutely true. Cupid's arrow found my heart. Lisa was the girl for me.

"Help with what?" Lisa asked.

Good question. "I don't know. Whatever you're doing."

"Setting the stage for tomorrow's matinee," she said. Since I'd never heard Lisa talk much to anyone else, I figured she was as quiet as me. But maybe she was just waiting for an opening, waiting for someone to take interest. "Oh, you know what you could do, if you wanted? Collect the sherry glasses and we'll take them backstage for a wash."

I felt weird about going backstage, like the actors would yell at me. They didn't have their own individual dressing rooms, just a partially closed-off space with a row of desks and mirrors along the wall. Lisa picked up their costumes off the floor while they chatted and took off their makeup. The two men had their shirts off, and one of the women was in her bra and panties. We were like ghosts, to them. We didn't exist.

"Call time tomorrow is one o'clock," Lisa said, and the actors looked at her in the mirror, nodding their assent.

"Oh, Lisa!" said the woman in the bra. "I almost forgot, the hem of my dress caught on my shoe..."

"I noticed," Lisa said, ushering me and my dishes to the laundry tub in the corner. "Did it rip?"

The actress looked genuinely concerned. "Yeah, it did. Sorry. Can you sew it up before tomorrow?"

"That's my job."

Lisa seemed almost happy about the repair.

I was about to ask where I could find dish soap when one of the shirtless men asked, "Who's your little friend?"

You can only stay invisible for so long, I guess.

"She's FOH," Lisa said.

More codes I didn't understand. I told them, "I'm just a volunteer."

The actors surprised me by saying, "That's great" and "Thank you" and "*Sisters* couldn't survive without people like you." They really seemed to mean it, and that made me feel like a valuable contributor to the theatre. I smiled the whole time I washed their sherry glasses.

After every shift, I stuck around and helped Lisa backstage. She started calling me her "official unofficial Assistant SM," which had a nicer ring to it than "FOH." I'd worked up the courage to ask what exactly that stood for, and it was "front of house:" ushers, program hander-outers, people who worked with the public.

I'd worked up the courage to ask Lisa a lot of questions, actually. Even some pretty personal stuff. By the time we'd known each other for three or four months, our lives were twining. After work was done, she'd drive me home so I wouldn't have to take the streetcar at night. Around Christmas, I invited her up to see my tree. It was after midnight, but we sat together on my couch, drinking hot chocolate and eating ginger biscuits.

When she set her mug on my coffee table, I knew she wanted me to kiss her. Lisa was kind of transparent that way. I guess we both were. Love is hard to hide.

In that moment, I wasn't thinking about the cruel jabs I'd overheard from other volunteers. I didn't care what Lisa had between her legs. Sure I wondered if she was pre-op, or post-op, or non-op, or something else altogether, but it made no difference. I was totally besotted with her, and when her lips met mine I was as drunk.

We didn't go to bed together. Not that night. That night, we kissed by the magical fairy light of my Christmas tree. By one in the morning, Lisa walked dizzily out my door and called me the minute she stepped through hers. We talked until three, and fell asleep on our phones.

I didn't want to strip her, and I didn't want to ask. But I wanted to know. I wanted to know not only what lived between her thighs, but whether she liked *sex*, whether she liked *me*. I guess I should have known by then, but there's something about love that makes a person self-conscious and totally neurotic.

When we finally found our way to nudity, we found it in the dark. I never expected it to happen the way it did. We'd just finished tidying the makeshift dressing room when Lisa snapped off the light. Everyone else had gone home by then. We were the

68

last two people in the building. Lisa found me in the darkness and kissed me into submission, tearing into my pants. When she stroked me over of my panties, my knees buckled the same way they had the first time I saw her.

I fell at her feet, and she obviously took that as a sign, because she unzipped her pants. The stretchy satin of her panties kissed my cheek. When she'd pushed those down too, I brushed my lips across her pubic hair. It tickled my nose, but I didn't laugh. I didn't even laugh when her erection whacked the underside of my chin.

I bowed to her hardness, finding her wet tip with my bottom lip. She hissed in a way that sounded surprised, and her cock pulsed against my face. When I opened my mouth, she found her way inside, and the darkness subsided. I knew how to do this. I knew she wanted it. We both did.

Lisa was the whole package, with a cherry on top.

Everyone at the theatre must have known we were a couple, because the other volunteers stopped talking to me. If I liked Lisa, they didn't like me. That sort of thing. But I was lost in love and I didn't care what they thought.

During performances, instead of sitting in the house with the patrons, I'd sneak into Lisa's booth and watch her work. Her job seemed complicated, but she said she'd been doing it long enough that it felt simple. She worked with a prompt script in front of her—a big binder with the play's script in one column and her cues in another. The lighting and sound boards were huge panels with sliders that she often worked with both hands. I liked watching her fingers move.

The week *Sister in Sin* played host to a travelling drag show, I worried Lisa would expel me from the booth. It wasn't "her" show. It wasn't an in-house production they'd rehearsed over the course of a month, where she knew the play inside-out. For the travelling drag show, she was handed a playlist of karaoke tracks and lighting effects the performers wanted. I figured she'd have to focus.

That night, I stood at the back of the house instead of invading Lisa's glass booth. I didn't want to break her concentration. Instead, I inadvertently broke her heart.

At intermission, she came out in a huff. She saw me, but she didn't smile. I followed her toward the stage, but I was supposed to help sell soft drinks in the lobby. It wasn't until the tail end of intermission that I met her at the booth and asked, "What's wrong?"

"I could ask you the same question," she said.

"I don't get it," I said. "Why are you mad at me?"

"*Me*? Mad at *you*?" She cackled.

When Lisa entered the booth, I followed. I had no idea what was going on. "Did I do something wrong?"

She looked at me like she didn't know how to respond. Then she looked at her watch and said, "No time." Falling into her chair, she lowered the house lights and got the mirror ball spinning before turning on the karaoke track and illuminating the duo on stage.

"Do you hate drag queens?" I asked. Maybe that was the issue.

Her expression changed from driven to perplexed. "No. Why?"

"I don't know. Some people do, especially feminists and trans women, and feminist trans women."

"Drag queens are fine. I've got nothing against them." Lisa had her eyes on the show, but at least she was speaking to me. "I guess the only thing that bothers me is when the general population confuses people who identify as transgender with drag performers who are just putting on a show."

"That makes sense."

"It's a spectacle, after all. It's a music concert." Lisa glanced back at me. "They're nice guys, these two. But they are *guys*."

"Oh." I set my hand on her shoulder and felt the tension in her muscles relax. "I thought maybe that's why you were in a bad mood."

"I was in a bad mood because you've been avoiding me all night."

"What? No!" I couldn't believe she thought that. "I was staying out of your way so you could focus on your work."

She laughed, shaking her head, and her blonde ponytail whipped side to side. "Focus on *this* show? It's easy as pie." She glanced at me and smirked. "Mmm... *pie*."

I wasn't standing far away. The booth was small enough that we could never be farther than an arm's length from one another. But I'd never seen that look on her face during a show. She always concentrated so hard on her work, and I just watched. That night, she was concentrating on me.

Lisa's fingers slipped from the lighting board. She cupped my pussy, out of the blue, and pulled me close. Nobody had ever touched me so forcefully. Until then, even Lisa had only petted me like a kitten. She'd build my arousal up before sinking down between my thighs, tossing me clear over that cliff.

This was different. She slid her hand inside my panties and squeezed by my crotch. *Squeezed* it. Her palm pressed hot against my clit while her fingertips dabbed at my cunt.

"Wait a sec," Lisa said, adjusting her sliders. "I need to do a few things here."

She reached up to pause the audio system, then brought up a lighting wash, and she did it all one-handed, without tearing her fingers out of my pants.

"You're crazy," I whispered. The booth was somewhat soundproof, with audio from the stage coming in through speakers, but I still worried about talking too loudly. What if someone in the audience turned around and spotted Lisa's hand in my pants? Anything was possible.

"Okay, we're good for another three minutes," Lisa said, rubbing her wet fingers over my clit. "How's that?"

"I can't believe we're doing this."

My knees buckled and she raised an eyebrow. "So tell me to stop."

I couldn't. I didn't say a word, only whimpered as she stroked my pussy. She was so self-assured that I wondered if her attitude might be turning me on even more than her powerful fingers rubbing my clit.

On stage, the drag queens were singing a song I'd never heard. It was upbeat and playful, and they were dancing with sun umbrellas. But Lisa wasn't looking at them. She was looking at me.

"You're about to fall over," Lisa said. "Don't tell me you're coming already?"

I nodded. My heart raced in time with my throbbing clit. It felt huge when she toyed with it—huge and swollen and tender and hot.

"Can you come before this song is over?"

"Yeah," I whimpered, rocking against her hand. It was so tight against my pussy, trapped inside my pants. I couldn't believe I was getting off on her like this. It seemed almost impersonal, like rubbing against a washboard or some other inanimate surface.

"You really think you can come in a minute?" Her teeth gleamed as she grinned.

"Sooner," I squealed, clutching her shoulder for support. She never stopped smiling as I fucked her hand.

"Do it," she whispered. "Come for me."

"I am!" I said, trying not to shriek. The lights in the booth were dim, but if someone in the audience turned around and really looked, they'd see us. They'd see my embarrassing orgasm face while my thighs clenched and my calves seized and my whole body shuddered relentlessly.

"Quiet," Lisa hissed.

"I know!" I *was* being quiet, I thought, but I bit my lip to keep quieter.

"Quiet," Lisa whispered, like a tease, as my knees quaked.

It was too much, too much raw sensation. Her hand slid out of my pants as I tumbled to the rough industrial carpet.

"What are you doing down there, hmm?" Lisa's skin glowed bluish in the booth's weird lighting. "Getting hungry?"

"Yes. Please." It hadn't occurred to me before then, but once she planted that seed I could almost taste her on my tongue. "Are you sure you can concentrate on work if I go down on you?"

"Let's find out," she said, guiding my head between her legs.

The way Lisa's little booth was set up, the lighting board and all that stuff was set on a desk that ran from one wall to the other. And me? I was kneeling underneath that desk, with my chin on her chair, pawing into her pants.

"I can't believe we're doing this." I unzipped her fly, but the rest was tricky. I left it to her. "Aren't you afraid of getting caught?"

"Not afraid enough, I guess." Arching her ass off the chair, Lisa pulled down her pants. Her gaff was the tricky part—it was like a super-tight, super-strong pair of panties that she wore over her actual underwear. To keep everything in place.

Her panties came down just in time to catch her next audio cue. "Shit! Almost missed that one."

A queasy feeling came over me. "Maybe we shouldn't do this. I don't want to mess up the show."

"You won't," Lisa assured me. "If anyone messes it up, it'll be me."

"What if someone comes up here to see what's wrong? There's no lock on the door, and even with me hiding under the desk, they'll still know what's going on."

"Not if you keep quiet and stay between my legs," Lisa countered. And maybe she was right. Maybe, even with someone spying from the doorway, we'd get away with it.

Lisa's naughty parts weren't shy around me. Her cock slid eagerly from the space in her pelvis where she'd tucked it away. Its glistening tip found my lips like we were magnetized. I kissed it sweetly, and she sighed.

SEXY SURPRISES FOR CHRISTMAS

"Is that what you want?" I whispered, before kissing all the way up her shaft. Lisa wasn't especially hard yet, but I'd get her there. "Should I just kiss you all night?"

"No, no, no," Lisa moaned, probably a little louder than she'd intended. "Suck it, sweety."

Her hand slipped off the lighting board and landed heavily on my head. There wasn't much space down there. Good thing I wasn't claustrophobic or afraid of the dark.

As Lisa worked her magic with light and sound, I wrapped my lips around her engorged cockhead. She moaned as her precum spilled across my tongue, salty and sweet.

"I'm not distracting you?" I asked with her tip sitting gently in my mouth.

Under the long desk, Lisa wrapped her big hand around the back of my head. She pulled me in tighter between her spread legs, driving her erection into my throat. I gagged and she released her hold on me, but I didn't draw back. I whimpered, subjecting myself to the sweet pain until my eyes watered.

"Oh, honey," Lisa groaned. "Yes, just like that."

I couldn't see her. I wanted to look up into Lisa's face, see lust in her brilliant blue eyes, her pouting pink lips parting the way they do when she's truly aroused. But the damn desk was in the way. All I could do was imagine the sweet look on her face as I consumed her cock.

"I love it when you go crazy on me." Her voice was keen and hoarse. "Do it, honey. Go crazy."

Lisa always said stage managers had a presence about them that was both understated and commanding. In that moment, the understated went out the window and all that was left was the commanding. If Lisa wanted crazy, that's what she'd get.

Wrapping my fist around her firm shaft, I sucked the tip as it spilled precum all across my tongue. That sweet juice made me suck harder, faster, jerking her off with one hand while I fucked her with my face.

"Oh God, I can hardly hear the music." Lisa's thighs shook. Her balls pulled up tight to her body, so my thumb whacked it as I stroked her hot and fast.

"Come," I said around her cock. "Come in my mouth, baby."

"My hands are shaking. My fingers..." They landed in my hair, her short fingernails digging into my scalp, making me crazy. "You *are* distracting, honey. I'm going to lose my job. I'm going to lose my mind!"

"Come!" I squealed, working harder to get her there.

"In less than a minute, I've got to three lighting cues, back to back to back." Lisa gasped as I hit a sweet spot with my tongue. "Oh honey, I'm shaking all over."

I drew back quickly. "Can't do your job with shaking fingers." God, I wished I could see her beautiful face. "Better come fast, baby."

"You just try and stop me," Lisa grunted, bucking so wildly her chair squealed.

Her fingers clenched in my hair and she pulled it hard enough to hurt before she stopped moving altogether. Her cockhead pulsed against my tongue. She whimpered like a puppy as she flooded my mouth with hot cream. It slid down my tongue, and it was gone before I got a good taste.

Another blast rushed my mouth, and I savoured this one before I missed it completely. Lisa's cum tasted incredible—sweet, tangy, and light as meringue. I loved it.

She started to giggle, "Enough," pushing my head away. "Oh, you're killing me, sweetheart. How am I supposed to work like this?"

"You asked for it," I said with a self-satisfied smirk she couldn't see. I was sitting on my feet, under her desk, with my back against the wall. It was dark, and all I could hear now was the music fading away.

I crawled around Lisa's chair to watch as she fiddled with her sliders. The stage went from peachy keen to pool party, all because of her lighting effects. When the performers finished their shtick, Lisa pulled up the volume on the next track. It was a song I recognized, but not well enough to name or sing along. I wasn't really up on popular music.

But the audience definitely was. As the drag queens danced through the intro, the whole audience broke out in applause. When the chorus arrived, everybody sang along. Even Lisa joined in, though she sang quietly enough that only I could hear.

I wrapped my arms around her neck and rocked her side to side. Watching our reflections in the dark glass of the booth window, I kissed her hair.

"You're cute," I said, and she rolled her eyes. "What? You are."

Her cheeks burned crimson, but she only stopped singing long enough to say, "Thanks."

© 2014 Giselle Renarde

Tie a Red Silk Ribbon

"**I**'m not good with gifts," he said, flipping through the jewellery store flyer. "You'll have to tell me what you want, otherwise it'll be a gift card like last year—and you didn't seem too impressed by that."

"I keep telling you," she replied. "I don't want any gifts. All I want is you!"

The corner of his mouth rose in a dimpled smile that drove her attention to the dark stubble of his cheek. Previously, she'd been focused on the loosely attached robe—or, rather, the generous hint of muscular thigh visible through the glass-top breakfast table.

"I have to give you something," he told her.

"You give me plenty, babe."

Approaching him slowly, she ran her hands through his thick hair, which had been warmed by the winter sun filtering in through the skylight. His hair was wonderful. And his neck, and his shoulders. She couldn't stop touching him.

He gave a nervous laugh, and said, "If you don't slow down, you'll have to finish what you start."

"Oh I will, will I?" she teased.

Fluttering into the front hall, she grabbed a silk scarf and returned to him in the kitchen. He hadn't moved except to turn his chair on an angle, presumably so she could straddle him easily without banging any portion of her anatomy against the glass table.

"What's that you've got there?" he asked.

"A ribbon," she replied. "To wrap my gift."

He didn't need to ask what she meant. He opened his robe to reveal an interested third party, and she sped forward to cradle his balls in silk. She could only imagine how good it felt by his grateful moan.

When she started wrapping the red scarf around the base of his erection to create a delightful package, he nervously asked, "Whatcha doin there?"

"Just wrapping my gift."

She tightened the scarf and tied a lovely red bow at the base of his cock.

"Not too tight," he begged, but clearly it was too late to make that request. She'd circled the silk scarf expertly around his ever-growing girth. Now that she'd tied a bow around it, it was her gift to receive. Only she could unwrap it.

"Oh God," he said, staring down at his dick. "Look what it's doing."

She raised an eyebrow. She knew she'd get a reaction, but she hadn't expected it to be so immediate. The scarf tied around his shaft served as a cock ring, trapping his hard masculine passion right where she wanted it.

"You've never looked so huge," she cooed.

"I've never been so huge!"

With an amused smirk, she wrapped her fingers around his incredible hardness.

As he threw his head back with an aroused groan, she asked, "Should I unwrap my gift now? Or wait until Christmas?"

You might also enjoy:

The Red Satin Collection
By Giselle Renarde
Winner of the 2012 Rainbow Awards
BEST TRANSGENDER ROMANCE

COMING HOME MEANS COMING out...

This is a Christmas of firsts for girlfriends Maisie and Regan. Maisie hasn't returned to their hometown since beginning her transition from male to female. Regan hasn't spoken to her hard-drinking Cree father in twice that time. Will family drama, secrets, and new arrivals strengthen their bond or tear Regan and Maisie apart?

The Red Satin Collection is a transgender lesbian holiday romance that includes content suitable for adult readers only.

ABOUT THE AUTHOR

G iselle Renarde is an award-winning queer Canadian writer. Nominated Toronto's Best Author in NOW Magazine's 2015 Readers' Choice Awards, her fiction has appeared in well over 100 short story anthologies, including prestigious collections like Best Lesbian Romance, Best Women's Erotica, and the Lambda Award-winning collection Take Me There, edited by Tristan Taormino. Giselle's juicy novels include Anonymous, Cherry, Seven Kisses, and The Other Side of Ruth.

Giselle Renarde
Canada just got hotter!
Want to stay up to date? Visit
http://donutsdesires.blogspot.com[1]!
Sign up for Giselle's newsletter: http://eepurl.com/R4b11
Weekly Audio Erotica at http://Patreon.com/AudioErotica

---

1. http://donutsdesires.blogspot.com/

GISELLE RENARDE

2

Milton Keynes UK
Ingram Content Group UK Ltd.
UKHW020237301123
433483UK00016B/828